Max's Dragon Shirt

· ROSEMARY WELLS ·
Max's Dragon Shirt

SCHOLASTIC INC.
New York Toronto London Auckland Sydney

For Atha

ISBN 0-590-12698-9

12 11 10 9 8 7 6 5 4 3 2 1   7 8 9/9 0 1 2/0

Printed in the U.S.A.   09
First Scholastic printing, September 1997

Designed by Atha Tehon. The full-color artwork for each picture was prepared using pen and ink line and watercolor on paper. It was color-separated and reproduced as red, blue, yellow, and black halftones.

Max loved his old blue pants more than anything.
"Those pants are disgusting, Max," said Max's sister, Ruby.

"We're going to the store to buy you a pair of brand-new
　pants," Ruby said.
"Dragon shirt," said Max.
"No, Max," said Ruby. "Mother only gave me five dollars
　to buy pants. After that there will be no money left."

On the way up to Boys' Sportswear
Ruby saw a red dress that she absolutely loved.

She thought she would try it on just for fun.
It was too tight.
Ruby wanted to find another dress.

"Wait there and don't move," said Ruby.

"Dragon shirt," said Max.

"Max," said Ruby, "after we buy your new pants, we'll have no money left."

Ruby put on a green dress.
It was too big.
"Stay here for just a minute, Max," she said.

Then she came back with a purple dress.
The purple dress was ugly.
"I'll be right back, Max," said Ruby.

After a while Max woke up.
Ruby was gone.

He went to look for her. He saw her yellow dress
and followed it out of Girls' Better Dresses...

into Hats...

and then into Boys' Sportswear, where he found a dragon shirt.
"Dragon shirt, please!" Max asked Ruby.

But it wasn't Ruby in the yellow dress.
It was a teenager.

Max screamed.

Back in Girls' Better Dresses Ruby heard it.
She ran to the changing room. Max was gone.

Ruby could not see him anywhere.

She went down the escalator to Makeup.
"Have you seen a little boy in blue pants?"
Ruby asked the perfume lady.
"No," said the perfume lady, "but I have some nice blue perfume."

"Are you looking for a vacuum cleaner?"
asked the man in Large Appliances.
"No," said Ruby. "I'm looking for a little boy in blue pants."

Ruby went up the escalator to Boys' Sportswear.
"Max, where are you?" she shouted.
"Are you looking for someone?" asked the saleslady.

"I'm looking for a little boy in blue pants," said Ruby.

"I saw a little boy in a green shirt," said the saleslady.

"He was looking for his sister in a yellow dress."

"That's me," said Ruby.

"No, it isn't," said the saleslady.

"That's a purple dress if I've ever seen one."

The saleslady made Ruby put on her own dress.
Then she took her down the escalator to the restaurant.
"Your brother could use a new pair of pants," said the saleslady.
"Boys' pants are only five dollars a pair this week."

Max was eating ice cream with two policemen and the teenager. There was chocolate, strawberry, and pistachio ice cream all over the dragon shirt.

"That's a five-dollar shirt," said the saleslady.

Ruby had to buy it.

"No money left!" said Max.

Rosemary Wells is the acclaimed author of over fifty books for young children, most of which she has also illustrated. Her eight pioneering Very First Books about Max and Ruby (all published by Dial) were applauded by *School Library Journal* as "a four-star performance . . . bound to be early childhood favorites." Her *Voyage to the Bunny Planet* trilogy (Dial) was called a "classic in the making" by *U.S. News and World Report*. Her most recent series for Dial, Edward the Unready, was praised by *Newsweek* for being "so touching, it will give you heart palpitations." Mrs. Wells lives in Westchester County, New York.